Ch
to
Re:

CW00854988

Written by
Steffi Gardner

Copyright © Stefanja Gardner 2020

CHARLIE TO THE RESCUE

ISBN 9798559346311

Other books from Steffi Gardner

Non fiction books

For Love of Harry
Life with Harry

Children's fiction

Charlie's Quest

To contact the author,
email: steffig@gmx.com

Charlie
to the
Rescue

Steffi Gardner

With acknowledgment and thanks to
Lynn Stuart and Tatyana Croci

CHAPTERS

Beginnings

Charlie was born different. He was a black and white Border Collie, similar to his brothers and sister but what you noticed about him was his appearance, which was slightly different! He had one ear which stuck up whilst the other lay flat against his head. However, the most striking feature was his eyes. One was blue – the other amber – almost green in certain lights.

There are lots of myths or legends in Pembrokeshire, where our story is set. The American Indians, sometimes called the First Nations, have myths too. They believe that people or animals with different coloured eyes are able to see both earth and heaven at the same time - which makes them very special indeed.

During a general health check at the vets Mr and Mrs Jenkins who owned the farm where the puppies were born asked about Charlie's ear.

'What about Charlie's ear?' they asked. 'Is it going to stay like that?'

Mr Mason the vet looked surprised. 'There's nothing wrong with it' he exclaimed. 'He can hear just as well as his siblings. Just imagine there were four of you inside your mum. You'd be cramped too. He just got a little squashed.

'Squashed' Mrs Jenkins said, concern in her voice. 'Are you saying we've got a squashed puppy?'

'No, he's fine really. He'll be as right as rain' said the vet beaming at Charlie and giving him a friendly scratch. Charlie knew there was nothing wrong with his hearing because when the pups were called for their food, he heard that just fine. So what if his ear was squashed it was just one of those things. After all people are all different too so why not puppies?

The four pups were born in the farmhouse kitchen late one wild, stormy night and Charlie the last was thought to be the runt of the litter as he was the smallest, and took a very long time to be born. In fact, Mrs Jenkins was getting quite worried. "No more puppies for Mollie" she thought. "This is too much for her."

'As Mollie strained to give birth to her last puppy, she looked at Mrs Jenkins as if to say 'please no more'. That was it. As she comforted the mum, she promised her no more. It was as if Mollie understood. With a big sigh of relief, she whelped her last puppy.

He lay limp and unmoving. Was cold and blue. Mrs Jenkins wondered if he was dead, as he had taken so long to be born. In any other hands Charlie might not have stood a chance, but Mrs Jenkins after quickly seeing to Mollie, cleared the limp puppy's airway so he could breathe. She rubbed him down as hard as she dared and finding he was still cold popped him in a clean warm towel inside which was a small hot water bottle. Just the right temperature.

However, the pup still didn't move. I won't give up thought Mrs Jenkins. One more try. It was as she was rubbing him down for the last time that she thought she could see the vague shadow of a dog hovering nearby. She turned her head – nothing there! yet she sensed she was not alone. Weird that. 'I must be tired. I'll be talking to myself next'.

She concentrated on the puppy and had almost given up when out of the blue the pup seemed to come to with a gasp and a weak cry. He gave a little start and began to wriggle. 'Well I never' Mrs Jenkins said to herself, much relieved. 'I've seen it all. Thank goodness I persevered!'

Now, not everyone was as clever as Mrs Jenkins, but she was a farmer's wife and had plenty of experience in looking after newborns, whether they were lambs or puppies who had a difficult start.

After all, her grandparents and parents had been farmers all their lives, and from being small she had learned skills from them sometimes without being aware of it.

Mrs Jenkins therefore had a lot of knowledge and skills and knew exactly what she was doing and so Charlie survived.

He couldn't have been in safer or kinder hands, though of course he didn't know that at the time, or that he was not alone! 'It was almost like a miracle' Mrs Jenkins told her husband later that night when the children, Richard and Alys, were in bed. 'For one awful minute I thought we 'd lost him. This is what was weird though' and she went on to tell him about the shadow dog she thought she'd seen.
Her husband, Tony, roared with laughter.

'Go on, you must have been imagining it' 'You'll be saying fairies exist next, just like our Alys.' 'Who says they don't?' Mrs Jenkins replied. 'You believe in angels, you told me so, so if there are angels – why not fairies'? Mr Jenkins didn't know what to say, so wisely just drank his tea!

The Puppies

'Smells' Mollie told the pups when they were a few weeks' old 'are very important to a dog as unlike human babies their eyes do not open when they are born. It usually takes ten days or so before they begin to see'. With a good sense of smell though they can find mum and their brothers and sisters, but more importantly the food! Initially Mollie's milk.

At times with four energetic, hungry puppies to feed and clean-up Mollie was very tired and occasionally needed to get away for a little while but she never ever went far.

Especially those first important weeks. In the beginning Charlie didn't know why smells were so important but as he grew older, he began to think that dogs were much better than people. Why? Because they could smell loads and loads more things. Dogs had special scent things in their noses, receptors they were called, and guess what, they had four times as many as people. So, it was no competition really.

A person could smell they were having stew for lunch. So, could a dog, but a dog could tell you each item in that stew. Meat, carrots, potatoes, celery and spinach etc. You name it, they could smell it. When it came to people if only, they knew what they smelled like. PHEW!

Growing Up

Of the four pups Max was the largest, and from the beginning he was the most confident. Everyone could see that. Always the first to feed, and squirming and wriggling when he had to make way for one of his brothers or his sister, he soon found his way back to mum. Cassie was the second born.

Not as big as her brother but she could hold her own when it came to food. Pup number three was Toby. He was slightly smaller than the others and a little lazy. He always seemed to be sleeping, yawning or feeding and as he grew up would always try to get away with as little work as possible.

Then there was Charlie, the last born, who almost didn't make it! Perhaps that's why Mrs Jenkins had a soft spot for him. She loved a trier and he was certainly that. He may have been slow to start but as soon as he realised the back teats were the best for milk, he was there sucking for all he was worth, 'til replete, tiny amounts of milk frothed at the corners of his mouth. Sometimes when not snuggled up to his brothers and sister he would sleep on his back, all four paws in the air showing one little rounded tummy. Life was bliss!

Now when the pups were four weeks old, they were introduced to a little proper dog food; not just Mollie's milk. Nothing out of tins mind you! At six weeks it was mostly all dog food and cooked, blended vegetables with a few extras.

The food, as you can guess, was Mrs Jenkins' job. She and her husband Mr Jenkins, known to friends as Anne and Tony, ran the farm near the Pembrokeshire coast not too far as the crow flies from St David's.

You couldn't see the farm from the road. It was hidden down a narrow country lane and had been in Mr Jenkins' family for more than one hundred years.

To earn some extra money Mrs Jenkins ran the Bed and Breakfast side of the farm with the occasional help at week-ends and during the summer holidays from their two children Richard and Alys.
'Reckon those pups get better fed than I do
Tony Jenkins grumbled good-naturedly one morning – but that was just his little joke.

Certainly, everyone at the farm looked healthy and happy.

Once the pups were on their feet and walking and exploring, they played and fought with each other, as brothers and sisters sometimes do. However, when one of the pups was a little too rough and bit one of the others too hard it would yelp and fight back so they all learned that biting even when playing was not a good thing. They were disciplined by Mollie as well, of course. Good manners were important and who better to teach them than their mum, Mollie.

All in all, Mr Jenkins was delighted with the litter. He was heard to say that he thought there might be one or two champion sheepdogs in the making, though it was far too early to tell.

Life for the pups was good. They loved exploring where they were allowed to go, and in Charlie's case where he was not! Whereas all the others were happy to be in the kitchen when not outside with Anne, Tony and the children, Charlie wasn't. He always seemed to be on the go, racing round at top speed no matter where he was, and sniffing the air. At times he would just sit with his eyes closed, tongue hanging out smelling everything around him. Life was wonderful he thought. He longed to explore and if the door was open would dash outside and follow his nose. When he could manage it, he would also explore all the passages and rooms in the farmhouse including the bedrooms!

He knew very well puppies weren't allowed upstairs but somehow, he always forgot! He just couldn't resist those lovely smells no matter where they came from. Now this wasn't always a good thing as you can imagine but what treasures he would find. His favourites included socks, underpants, shirts, and from time to time jumpers, mostly the children's – the smellier the things the better.

When he found things, he would proudly carry his finds downstairs in his mouth.
Sometimes things like shirts were too big for him to carry so he would drag them down the stairs much to Mrs Jenkins' annoyance.
'You've left your bedroom doors open again' she would say when the children grumbled
'What have I told you about that?'
She even lost her temper a few times when the puppies who had found a shirt decided to play tag and sank their teeth into it and pulled. Rip would go the shirt and then there was trouble.
'Out to the barn with them' said Mrs Jenkins one day

when they had ripped a hole in Alys's new school shirt. 'I've had enough. They are big enough now to sleep outside.'

So off they went. They didn't really mind for as Max said it was warm. There were nice things to sleep on and to play with and as far as Charlie was concerned there were wonderful smells.

Moving On

Once Mrs Jenkins had fed the pups in the kitchen, four small meals a day, they were allowed outside in the yard as long as someone was with them. When not in the kitchen being fed or outside, they were to be found in the barn asleep.

Why do you think that was? One of the reasons was that they were still young and untrained. Can you think of anything else? A five-letter word beginning with 's and ending with p', that's right the word is sleep. Well done for guessing. Just as young babies tend to do this a lot so do puppies. They need it to grow big and strong.

One day when they were almost seven weeks' old, they were sitting outside in a special pen and could see their mother Mollie working a few sheep nearby. 'Let's try the pups one at a time' said Mr Jenkins to his wife. So, she handed him Max who was placed near his mum in the small paddock with four or five sheep nearby. The other pups looked on – this was different!

Mr Jenkins used a whistle and his voice to get Mollie to move the sheep, and the pup in with her soon realised what was happening. It was fun Max thought as he followed Mollie and tried to imitate her.

Mr Jenkins did the same with the other pups and all went well until it was Charlie's turn. He started off well until he smelled an entirely new scent on the breeze, then he stopped, sniffed the air and began to follow it, only stopping when he came to the gate. Then Mollie came racing up barking and herding him back. She was not pleased nor was Mr Jenkins.

The following day the pups tried out the herding game this time with the geese. It was fun! They stalked them as Mollie had done the sheep. 'Giving them the collie eye' this was called. A skill all good sheepdogs possess.

Over the next few days Max, Cassie and Toby decided to scatter the geese then round them up. What fun. They could play at this all day, but although at first Charlie enjoyed the game after a while, he became bored. "Geese were such silly creatures" he thought.

New Homes

When the pups were just over five weeks' old the telephone never seemed to stop ringing.

Mollie's pups had been advertised locally mainly by word of mouth. There was quite a lot of interest as all the farmers nearby knew each other and several farming friends of the Jenkins wanted to come and see the litter. A small ad had also been placed in the local paper under Livestock.

'Collie pups for sale. Excellent pedigree.
Working homes required'.

Several people on holiday who had seen the ad rang up. Some had even called round. They were looking for a pet! Fortunately, though Max, Cassie and Toby had already been provisionally booked, sight unseen, and if all went well would, when they were ready to leave, have working homes to go to. Although polite both Mr and Mrs Jenkins had turned away people who wanted a collie purely as a pet.

'No pet homes' said Mr Jenkins. 'I don't want that for my dogs. They come from good working stock, were bred to work and that's what they need to do.'

Anne and Tony had been talking and both agreed they would prefer the pups to go locally. 'That way I know where they are and importantly who they are with and what they are doing' said Mr Jenkins.

He had seen too many collies in the wrong homes, with the wrong people where they became bored, partly because their owners were out at work all day.

Then when problems came the people couldn't understand why the once playful puppy was turning into a very different character. 'Give them a job to do and put their brains to work – that'll keep dogs healthy and out of mischief. That's what my dad always used to say! I don't think he was far wrong - was he?'

He remembered that one or two puppies from a previous litter of Mollie's well over two years ago had been bought by people who did agility work with their dogs. That was ok as he knew the dogs were happy to be working and busy. On one or two occasions both he and Anne had watched agility competitions and were delighted to see the success achieved by puppies they had bred.

Everyone enjoyed the sport and it was easy to see the loving bond between owners and dogs.

Of course, this time, initially, people had come to see all four puppies but for some reason no-one wanted Charlie. By now you'll have probably guessed why! Unlike his brothers and sister and his appearance there was one big difference. As far as Charlie was concerned, he didn't like sheep.

Actually, that's not quite true! To be honest it wasn't that he didn't like them but he was just not interested in working them.

What to do with Charlie?

Mrs Jenkins worried about Charlie. Yes, he enjoyed occasionally playing at herding the geese, but when it came to the sheep – no thank you. It was as if his mind was on other things. She could see the pup was different from the others but hoped he would grow out of it. In this she was proved wrong.

Every day Charlie would sit and look at the sheep out of curiosity but as soon as he scented a smell on the breeze, off he went.

He was obedient and usually came back when called but it was clear to see what really interested him. His brothers and sister could not understand him. They liked sheep but with Charlie it was smells.

Now his mother Mollie was also worried as was Charlie's dad Sky. 'What are we going to do with him?' 'Don't ask me' said his dad. Sky was a well-known sheepdog and over the years at trials had won many prizes. As had Mollie.

It was one of Mrs. Jenkins' jobs to polish all the trophies the dogs had won. She polished them until they shone and put them on the mantelpiece surrounding the fire where they gleamed in the light.

All their rosettes had been framed and put in the hall for everyone to see.

Sky was in his prime and worked very hard and was well able to put the youngsters in their place and show them how the job should be done if he thought they were slacking.

However, neither Mollie nor Sky knew what to do with Charlie. In fact, one night his dad had shaken his head and sighed saying 'Charlie what on earth are we going to do with you?' Charlie had looked at his parents then turned away, his tail between his legs as he went back to the barn and lay down. I'm useless he thought. I have no purpose, no wonder mum and dad don't love me. But he was wrong. They did love him just as much as the others but had no idea what to do.

Anne and Tony Jenkins also talked about Charlie. Never had they had a sheepdog that didn't want to work sheep. 'Why don't you try one to one training again, see if that makes a difference.' Mrs Jenkins suggested. Mr Jenkins tried it encouraging Charlie with Mollie to round up several sheep but the dog just sat there watching him as if waiting for an entirely different command.

Very occasionally Sky watched. He had a feeling deep in his bones that he knew who Charlie took after. Long, long ago when he was just a pup himself, he was sure he had heard his own mother talking about a distant relative of theirs. That dog had never wanted to be a sheepdog, but had done great things in an entirely different field.

It was something to do with people but Sky couldn't exactly remember what. After all it was a very very long time ago and he wasn't entirely sure if it wasn't just one of the stories his mother used to tell them when they too were small.

Although Sky loved all his puppies, at the same time he felt slightly embarrassed that Charlie wasn't like the others. He didn't want to think there was anything wrong with any of them. Do you think he was right? However, late one night when Charlie's parents were talking about how well the others pups appeared to be doing and how they would miss them when they went to new homes Mollie sighed.

'I've been thinking' she said. 'Just because Charlie is different it doesn't mean there is anything wrong with him. 'I'm sure he is as clever as the others – he just thinks differently'. Let's wait and see.' In the end she was proved right but that is in the future.

Changes

It was clear by ten weeks of age Charlie was not
sheepdog material and, in all honesty, couldn't be sold
as such. What use would he be as a sheepdog? He
was very interested in everything that was going on
around him, people, tractors, the sounds on the farm,
strange smells, and even at times the geese etc with one
exception. Sheep.

Richard and Alys, the farmer's children were quite
fond of Charlie. Sometimes they would play hide and
seek with him and he always found them because of
their particular smells. Their friends too if he wanted
to. Some of them however were not very kind. 'Look
at his peculiar eyes' they would say, and 'isn't he weird.'
Charlie wasn't sure what people were saying but he
knew they were talking about him and making fun of
him and at times it made him sad.
Sometimes he didn't even want his food.

He thought what's the use of being a dog. 'I don't fit in.
I've no job to do?'

Rosie who was Alys's best friend at school never made fun of Charlie because she loved him. She kept wishing her parents would buy him for her but her mum liked cats, and when she asked her dad, he said that she was too young for a dog.

By now Charlie was on his own the other pups having gone to new homes. He did miss them and hoped they were happy. He thought again about what Mollie had said to him the other day that he was special - 'but how can I be special, when I don't know what I'm supposed to do?' he wondered. 'There must be something – but what?' Surely someone will want me?' At times at night he would dream of finding the perfect home and occasionally he felt someone whispering in his ear 'just be patient, not too long now.'

He felt he saw a doggy shape occasionally and he could smell something - but it wasn't very clear. 'Just a dream' he thought and said nothing to anyone. It was odd though that his nose would twitch when having the dream.

Mr & Mrs Jenkins were honest with all who came to see Charlie. 'Yes, he has an excellent pedigree but shows absolutely no interest in working sheep whatsoever. Must be a throwback somewhere but we don't know where.' So, time went by and Charlie grew bigger, and bigger. He still had one ear up and the other mostly down.

He still loved different smells until even with his eyes closed, he knew exactly where he was and more importantly where he could find the smells.

Sometimes on a Saturday or during school holidays Rosie would come over to spend time with Richard and Alys, but Richard soon got bored so it was left to the two girls to find things they both enjoyed.

One of these was hiding from Charlie and calling to him to find them. More often than not he would come but when he found something more enticing, he would not always respond so then the girls would go and look for him. The only time he would always come back was if he knew the girls had something good to eat.

Charlie knew everything by smell now and knew Rosie didn't smell the same as the twins. It didn't matter what clothes she wore; he always knew when she was about.

Something else also happened when she was near; his little nose would start to twitch.
Very peculiar!

The Stranger

One cold morning when the children were at school, and Charlie was lying on the kitchen floor sulking the phone rang.

Mrs Jenkins who was baking wiped her hands and went to answer it. Earlier that morning while exploring Charlie had somehow managed to fall into the slurry pit, with a splosh.

Slurry spurted everywhere, all over his body, his feet were covered in it, but as luck would have it not his eyes. He could smell himself, and boy did he pong! 'I must get out' he said to himself, but the sides were too steep and he couldn't.

Fortunately, Richard happened to be in the farmyard and heard a glump, glump sound coming from the slurry pit. He tried to hook Charlie out with a big stick he found nearby but couldn't reach him. As luck would have it just at that moment his dad drove up.

'Dad' Richard yelled 'Charlie's fallen in the slurry pit and I can't get him out.'

Charlie was hauled out by a furious Mr Jenkins. The dog was covered in slime but didn't appear to be any worse for his ordeal.

He shook himself and the slime went everywhere, spattering both Mr Jenkins and his son.

'It wasn't my fault' Charlie said to himself as a furious Mr Jenkins hosed him down in the yard before chaining him up. He and Richard dashed into the house to change, throwing their smelly clothes into the washing machine.

'That was bad enough' thought Charlie but worse was to come, as Richard told his mum what had happened and asked if he could have a towel to dry Charlie. 'That dog is not coming in here his mother said. He stinks to high heaven. 'The shivering little soul looked pitifully at her and she sighed and relented.

However, she insisted Charlie had another wash - this time with shampoo and in the downstairs shower. As the water cascaded over him and the shampoo was rubbed well in then rinsed off Charlie wriggled. 'I hate this shampoo' he said to himself. It's stinky and smells girly. Now washed, dried and combed he was confined to the kitchen to dry off safety. 'It wasn't my fault I slipped' he thought again.

The farmhouse kitchen had a grey slate floor and though the cooker, a large Aga, was on, Charlie lay nose tucked into his tail. He longed for the old kitchen with its big settee, his favourite place to curl up.

However, Mrs Jenkins had wanted a new kitchen with a slate floor etc, and Charlie's old settee had to go.

Charlie said to himself that it might be a more modern kitchen but it wasn't as cosy as the old one with its rug and settee. He did not understand why SHE couldn't have kept things as they were. It had been so comfy and smelled wonderful. In its place now was a large table and six chairs though to be fair Mrs Jenkins had kept the rug. This was now in the washing machine spinning round in the wash as Mrs Jenkins had said it was getting smelly. Charlie had disagreed. It had been just right!

Charlie started to relax and began to dream – such a lovely dream, when the phone rang. He could see himself fully grown, both ears down but just as the picture came unto his mind, he heard his name. Head cocked on one side he tried to hear what was being said.

'You are welcome to come and have a look. We've reduced the price because he really has to go as we don't need another dog, especially one that won't work sheep.'

Mrs Jenkins came over to Charlie dog brush and comb in hand. 'Now Charlie – time for a brush and comb. We have a visitor coming.'

Charlie wasn't a great lover of being brushed, or being clean and tidy come to that. When he saw Mrs Jenkins came towards him, he tried to escape, but there was nowhere to hide So, with tail down, he resigned himself to the inevitable.

Changes Afoot

The doorbell rang and Mrs Jenkins went to answer it. Into the room came a tall stranger.

A man. Charlie growled and shrank away, trying to hide behind Mrs Jenkins, who said 'he's not normally like this'

'I'm strange to him' said the man talking quietly 'it's natural for him to be wary – he's just summing me up and taking his time.' He sat down and Mrs Jenkins made them both a cup of tea. Mr Harries she called him. Charlie noticed that the man's movements were slow, even when he went to his coat pocket and his voice was kind. He smelled of fresh air and the outdoors, and!

Something smelled good! Food! Mr Harries pulled out a small round biscuit which he threw on the floor ignoring the dog completely.

Charlie slowly came forward, sniffed the biscuit then ate it. Nice. Very tasty. He waited to see if there was another but all the time kept his distance. He could smell there were more treats and waited. Nothing.

Maybe if he sat! 'Good boy' said Mr Harris and another treat came Charlie's way. This time Charlie ran to get it. He liked this – it was a good game.

He sat and looked at the man wondering what would happen next.
'How old is Charlie now?' Mr Harries asked.
'Nearly six months' was the answer.
'Is he fit?'
'As far as I know' came the answer.
Mr Harries, whose first name was Bob, asked what else could Mrs Jenkins tell him about Charlie.
'Does he play with balls for instance?'
'The children sometimes kick or throw a ball about and he will chase it and bring it back. He seems keen enough on that' said Mrs Jenkins.

'OK, let's see'. Mr Harries pulled a small tennis ball out of his coat pocket and bounced it up and down on the spot. He was going to throw the ball but then looked at Mrs Jenkins' face and decided not to risk it.

She didn't look that pleased! So, they all went outside where Mr Harries threw the ball – not that far away and when Charlie picked it up and brought it back, he was told what a good boy he was. Charlie was given another treat. 'Now let's see if you will go further' and Charlie did.

Back in the house Mrs Jenkins looked at Mr Harries. 'Why is it important that Charlie likes balls?'
They are allowed to play with them for a while, as a reward for finding someone.' He continued 'it's how we train'

He carried on talking. 'I work with Search and Rescue. I'm a volunteer. In fact, we all are. As you know sometimes people get lost on the hills or mountains or wander away and then we are tasked to go out with our dogs and find them. At times it is extremely difficult and bad weather doesn't help. We are always on the lookout for a dog with a little something extra about him to train up for this type of work.'

He continued. 'Normally we like dogs to start their training when they are about four months old. Some groups take them older than that. We just do a little each day.

Starting with some basic obedience work.
Nothing too strenuous and only in very short bursts as initially the important thing is to build up a bond of trust between dog and handler.

Charlie is a little older but he looks bright and I think he may well be what we are looking for. I have to be honest Mrs Jenkins and say we don't have much money to spend on buying our dogs. Often, they are given to us, though occasionally we will buy one, and sometimes we will take on a failed Police Dog.'

'How do you mean failed?'

'Occasionally a dog doesn't make the grade – it could be they are not outward going enough for the hard work police dogs do, or just not suited temperament wise but they might well be good for search and rescue work.'

He sipped his tea. 'We have had some fine ones in the past but at the moment we haven't anything new coming through, so we need to start training up some younger ones.

As I said, training is done in easy stages with rewards along the way, one of which is time out for the dog to play with a ball.'

Charlie is all Ears

Charlie listened. "I'm not sure what this Search and Rescue is he thought, but it sounded interesting especially if it involved playing with a ball". He decided he liked the smell of this man and also what he had in his pockets. Biscuits were fine but he preferred small dried pieces of liver. Also, he knew all the smells on the farm in each season off by heart now but unless in the kitchen he was usually tied up so he would not wander off and go exploring. A lone dog in areas where there were sheep was not a good thing. He listened again as Mrs Jenkins asked more questions.
'How long does training take?

'It varies' was the answer. 'Initially about six months, with little tests along the way, then longer as the dog gets better. In some truly exceptional cases top dogs can be in training for up to three years. It depends on what they are being trained to do and how long it takes them to learn.'

Another question. 'What happens if he doesn't make the grade?' Now Charlie was all ears. He didn't for one moment think he would fail. After all his mum said that he was bright maybe even brighter than Max. 'Well, if it doesn't work out, and a handler decides not to keep the dog or there's another reason, then we would look for a suitable home for him. That takes time and we do contact some collie rescue societies, as ideally, we want to place a dog with someone who is used to collies and knows their ways, likes and dislikes.'

'Matching up dog and owner is not always easy, but we try our hardest.' Bob Harries continued. 'Not all societies work in exactly the same way but that's how our branch does it.' He went on to say that occasionally a dog doesn't bond as well with another Search and Rescue volunteer. There might be a personality issue, for instance a dog liking to be with a particular type of person.

Mrs Jenkins nodded. She had seen often enough a mismatch between dog and owner.

Both then suffered. She thought for a few moments. 'Would an agility home be considered? We have a few friends who do agility with their collies.'

Then when Mr Harries nodded said that she would talk the matter over with her husband that evening. She added that Charlie needed to be doing something rather than getting into mischief and that they really didn't want to keep him fond of him though they were. She added 'but it is important that he goes to the right home.'

'He'd have that with me for sure. This is my phone number' Bob Harries said. 'Talk it over with your husband and then give me a ring either way. I'm on holiday for another five days. This is the first time I've been to Pembrokeshire and I'd like to see as much as I can. Sometimes out of season is the best time to come. Then if everything is ok, I could collect him on my way home.'

With that he said goodbye and left.
Later that night the Jenkins talked the matter over and decided they would let Charlie go. 'Not for free of course.' Mr Jenkins said that in his experience most people didn't value anything that was given away, though there were exceptions, and after all he was fond of the dog even though he could be a nuisance at times.

The Telephone Call

So, Charlie was sold to a delighted Mr Harries. "What's going on!" thought Charlie. He didn't know exactly what was happening but sensed changes were on the way.

He lay in the barn thinking about the man, the treats, and the quiet firm voice. He thought again of the farm, Mr and Mrs Jenkins, the children and Rosie who was never too tired to play with him but he was also excited. Something different was happening. He could sense it in the air.

Back in the farmhouse the telephone rang and Mr Jenkins went to answer it. 'Sorry Phil if only you'd 'phoned yesterday. I know your Rosie is fond of him but we've just sold Charlie to someone else.'

That night Charlie told his mother what had happened earlier. All about the man, the biscuits, the ball. Mollie was a little sad. She knew it was a parting of the ways.

Charlie was the last of her puppies to go and secretly she had hoped he would find a new home nearby.

"What will be will be" she thought as she licked him saying 'now remember, we love you. Be good and work hard wherever you are.' 'Two more days then Charlie goes' said Mrs Jenkins to her husband the following morning over breakfast. 'I will miss him but it is time he moved on and it is nice to think he will be working and doing something really useful.'

Charlie who was in the kitchen having breakfast heard this and there was a part of him now that wished he wasn't going. He thought back to yesterday and remembered how Rosie had cried into his fur as she put her arms around him. He had whined and licked her face which made her cry even more. He had barked to show her he wanted to play but she just gave him a biscuit and turned away.

It was just after twelve on the Saturday morning, Charlie's leaving day. Richard and Alys were in the kitchen having an argument.

Richard had been asked to lay the table for lunch but said that this was girls' work but Alys and her mum had disagreed.
'We all do our share Richard' she said. 'You know that's

only fair – so come on this time it's your turn.' With a sigh and grumble Richard agreed and did as he was asked, putting out the knives and forks and spoons.

He could smell the bread and butter pudding in the oven and didn't want to miss out, which might happen if his mum told his dad that he hadn't wanted to help. Does Richard remind you of anyone? Someone who likes to do as little as possible if they can get away with it?

Then something happened – well, two things more or less at once! First of all, the doorbell rang and Bob Harries arrived. The whole family were getting ready to say their goodbyes to Charlie, the children sniffing slightly, as they hugged him, when the phone rang.

Mrs Jenkins answered it then called to her husband. 'Tony, come quickly. It's Rosie's mum. Rosie's missing. She thought Rosie was playing in her room but when she called her for lunch there was no reply. And when she went into her room it was empty.

Her mum wondered if she had come over to see Charlie one last time as she was so upset, he was going.' No-one though had seen her though so that's what Mrs Jenkins told her mum. 'OK I'll tell Tony. I'm sure he'll want to help' said Anne She turned to her husband 'Rosie's dad and some friends are going to go and look for her. 'Count me in' said her husband and he took the phone from his wife's hand and listened intently to what was being said.

'Where's everyone meeting?' was one of the questions asked. As he went to get his coat Bob Harries asked if he could join the party and was told an extra pair of eyes would be most welcome, so he went out to his car where his backpack was lying, picked it up off the back seat and brought it back in checking its contents.

Everything was there. A spare warm jacket, hat and gloves, high vis jacket. First Aid Kit, splints, strapping tape etc. Shoes were changed for a pair of sturdy walking boots.

Bob Harries mentioned to the Jenkins that all search and rescue volunteers were required to be advanced first aiders and that usually they worked in conjunction with their local mountain rescue team. The team would always be backing up the volunteers and would have a full medical kit which included a stretcher.

Mr Jenkins had heard there was a mountain rescue team which also covered Pembrokeshire though it was not based locally. He couldn't remember what they were called.

Outside the wind had started to rise which often happens near the coast and as everyone listened to the local forecast, they heard that heavy rain coupled with high winds was expected later in the day. The sky had also darkened. Not a day to be outside especially if you were lost and alone.

Richard and Alys asked their father if they could come and help in the search.
'No' said their dad. 'I don't want the worry of keeping an eye on you especially as the weather is turning nasty'.
'Rosie is our main concern. 'He told them 'Stay here with your mum but if there is any news you can contact me on the mobile number.'

Charlie has a good idea.

Now Charlie didn't know what was happening but he heard Mrs Jenkins mention Rosie and knew something was wrong. He sat, head cocked on one side, and his nose began to twitch.

He knew somewhere nearby was another dog - the shadow dog he sensed in his dream.

This dog was urging Charlie to go. It didn't matter he couldn't see the dog with his own eyes, he knew it was there! He barked. "Shh" said Mr Jenkins. 'Charlie be quiet'.

Bob Harries turned and looked at Charlie wonderingly. It was as if the dog knew what was happening. But, how could he? The dog looked at him, his gaze never leaving Mr Harries' face. "There's something weird going on" Bob Harries thought. This dog knows he is needed. Charlie barked again and was told 'be quiet'.

For a moment Mr Harries had the strangest feeling. He sensed the presence of another dog. "Ridiculous" he thought looking round. Charlie was the only dog there. Yet!

As the two men began to leave Charlie got to his feet and began to bark and bark and pace backwards and forwards. 'Take me with you' he wanted to say but no-one was listening.

So, he ran to the front door, stood by it and barked again and again, each time more loudly than before. 'What on earth's wrong with that dog?' said Mr Jenkins. 'I've never known him to be like this, it's almost as if he wants us to take him with us.'

'Perhaps we ought' said Mr Harries. Once out of the door Charlie ran to the Land Rover and stood there tail wagging and eyes on the two men. The door was opened. Charlie jumped in and sat quietly. 'Good boy' whispered the voice in his head.

He no longer barked but his tail thumped the seat of the car. 'Come on, come on' it seemed to say. 'Hurry up, hurry up, hurry up!'

The Search

The kitchen at Rosie's was crowded. It seemed everyone was there. The rescuers were bending over a local map and a plan was being made as to where to search. There were several routes the little girl could have taken to get to the Jenkins' farm and each had to be covered.

There was one route her dad had ruled out. Because that way led through a field with cows. Rosie had been told time and time again never to cut through fields with cows in them, especially if they had calves. It was far too dangerous.

The first thing Mr Jenkins did when arriving at Rosie's was to put the dog on a lead. 'Don't want you missing too' he mumbled to himself.

He then realised Charlie was no longer his and started to hand the longline to Mr Harries.
'No' he said. 'Right now, Charlie is used to you and he will work better if he stays with you'. Charlie looked from one man to the other – thinking!

Follow Your Nose

The police had been called and an officer hoped to be there soon with a sniffer dog.

Unfortunately, the police dog handlers in Rosie's county, Dyfed Powys, had a very large area to cover, and when the call came through those on duty were all out on another job quite a distance away.

One of the officers had been contacted and she and her dog had now been despatched to go to Rosie's. However, they would not be there for at least an hour and a half depending on the traffic. So, for the moment, Charlie was the only dog in the vicinity. A young, untrained dog at that.

It had been decided that Bob Harries would team up with Tony Jenkins and Charlie.

Being local Tony had knowledge of the area though of the two men Bob Harries was the person with the most experience of search and rescue. Rosie's dad was teamed up with a friend, as were the two other volunteers.

Mr Harries looked at Rosie's mum who was in tears. 'Will you allow Charlie to sniff one of Rosie's dresses' he asked. 'Something she often wears?' Her parents looked doubtful but her mum went upstairs and came down with a dress.

Charlie knew that dress very well. It smelled of Rosie. She had worn it when she last visited.
Her mum's voice shook and she was crying.
'I wouldn't let her go to see Charlie – said she had to stay at home and I sent her upstairs to play. She only has a dress and thin cardigan on. Her coat is hanging behind the door. Her boots are in the hall too. Please find her quickly. It has gone past lunch time.
She is diabetic and needs something to eat.
'Do you have any sugar cubes or a sandwich?' asked Bob Harries. 'Anything like that will do.' Sugar cubes were found and a couple of sandwiches quickly made and wrapped up. Everyone put something in their backpacks. He asked Rosie's mum if she had anyone who could come and stay with her while they were out? 'Yes' she said 'my cousin's on her way.' As she spoke a car could be heard drawing up outside.
The search party left, in pairs. Rosie's dad couldn't wait another minute. He couldn't bear to think his daughter was out there somewhere missing. Maybe hurt or worse.

Charlie to the Rescue

The area to be covered had been agreed upon before the men left. Mobile phones had been charged and were carried by everyone and though sometimes a signal might not be received the emergency number would always be activated.

The grey sky was looking ominous. It was becoming darker and darker. It was a miserable afternoon and even the men shivered. The wind was starting to grow stronger and the leaves were being blown backwards and forwards. The men kept checked in with one another. No signs of Rosie were found on the main road so it was thought she must have cut across fields. The men looked at their maps again and discussed the routes she could have taken.

'She won't have crossed those fields' said her father, 'I told her not to'. He said this in an angry voice as Charlie strained at the lead and began to whine. 'Do you think ......' Mr Harries began to say before he was interrupted by Rosie's dad. 'We are wasting time' he said.' 'I've told you she wouldn't go that way'. He was so worried that his voice sounded rough and slightly rude, but everyone understood. Still Charlie was whining and tugging at the lead, that way.' Mr Jenkins and Mr Harries looked at each. 'I wonder' said Tony Jenkins.' Animals are unpredictable. Yet he can smell something.'

Rosie's dad was saying they ought to try a side road. Often there were short cuts or minor roads leading to the same place and there was one to the Jenkins' farm Rosie might have taken. He and his family had occasionally walked to the Jenkins's but it was in the summer in good weather. Not on a day like this. A day when she was all on her own. Would she remember how to get there?

Why couldn't they find her?
Just then a message came through that the dog handler and her dog had arrived and would be joining up with one of the search parties. The police dog had sniffed an article of Rosie's and was on its lead. This was sheep country after all and not all police dogs were good around sheep and no-one wanted an accident to happen.

'Let's see where Charlie takes us' said Mr Jenkins. 'He's ace when it comes to smells'.

Useless as a sheepdog but he might just have something, and he knows Rosie so well.' Her dad agreed and the others went off. Mr Jenkins let out the longline. Charlie dashed ahead the two men following him more slowly.

The dog cast first one way then another, backtracking. Puzzled. Scents were coming from different directions. He was confused.
He paced backwards and forwards. Unsure for the moment.

Charlie suddenly stopped. Something wasn't right. He was uneasy. Have I failed he asked himself? Then he heard the words 'follow your nose, go on just follow your nose'.

The voice in his head was very faint but it gave him new heart, and the courage to carry on.

All of a sudden, his nose twitched and, on the breeze, was a faint but familiar smell.

Rosie had been here. He knew it without being told, He began to whine and pull even harder.
'Let him off' said Mr Harries. 'You've told me he'll come back when called so we've got nothing to lose and maybe everything to gain.'

With that Charlie raced ahead. Mr Jenkins hoped he was right and certainly the dog had smelled something. However, what if he has made a mistake and it is someone else, he thought and they lost precious time!

The rain that had been threatening now fell. It was heavy and oh so cold! The wind had dropped slightly but the sky was overcast and light was fading fast. They had to find Rosie and soon.

Although the ground was uneven Charlie was running fast, the two men coming up behind moving as quickly as they could. on the uneven surface. The grass was wet and neither man wanted to risk a fall. Charlie could definitely smell Rosie now even if he couldn't see her. The scent was strong. They passed a field with cows in it. 'She can't have come this way' thought Mr Jenkins. The dog must be wrong. He whistled to Charlie to come back but Charlie ignored him. He knew he was right. In the distance he heard the police dog bark. He too had picked up a scent.

Charlie quickened his pace. At the far end of the next field was a rusty five bar gate.

Charlie braked, his feet digging into the ground. On the gate was a small piece of material. Part of a dress. Rosie's dress. The voice in his head said 'Well done.

Charlie, well done.'

The voice of the police dog was getting louder but Charlie was determined to get there first. Rosie was his responsibility and it was his job to find her. The shadow dog that had been encouraging Charlie was now silent – had faded into the background, though his strength was still there. 'Charlie's found something' said Mr Harries holding up the tattered piece of Rosie's dress. A message had been passed to Rosie's dad who was on his way. He'd was running fast. He'd met a friend with a car and been given a lift. He was now only a field away.

Up ahead at the far end of the next field were several large oaks with deep roots spreading out. Most of the leaves had been shed and branches were bending and creaking in the wind. It was a ghostly sound, but was there enough room for someone to shelter! Especially a child?

Then Charlie saw her. She was lying on the ground curled up by the roots of a large oak. Her dress was dirty. Her cardigan torn. She was wet, shivering and crying.

Charlie barked several times as he raced up to her and licked her face. 'Oh, Charlie' she cried, 'you've found me, you've found me.' Her hands went around the dog's neck and she cried into his fur as Rosie's dad hurried up. 'He saved me daddy; Charlie saved me' she cried. 'He certainly did' said her father. There was a lump in his throat and tears in his eyes.

Rosie's dad wept as he picked her up and he hugged her to him as if he would never let her go. 'I've hurt my foot daddy' she said. 'I slipped and fell. The cows chased me and I was frightened.' By now Mr Harries had contacted one of the other groups who were with the police dog handler to let them know Rosie had been found and was safe. Rosie's dad phoned her mum and Rosie spoke a few words to her. 'I'm safe mummy. I'm with daddy and Charlie.'

Charlie was put back on his lead, praised and given a biscuit and Mr Harries after feeling Rosie's foot and saying he thought it was just a strain opened his backpack, and brought out several things, including a cube of sugar and a small sandwich. Rosie ate them eagerly.

From the pack came a special silver sheet which to Charlie looked very much like the silver foil Mrs Jenkins used when she cooked a chicken. Rosie was wrapped up in this, her foot checked and lightly strapped up.

Then her father carried her back down the field, through the gate to the nearest road where Rosie's dad's friend was waiting with his car. The dog handler and her dog were in the police car. The officer had been talking on the phone to headquarters and was now making notes, before getting out and expressing her relief that all was well.

No one seemed to notice the rain. All they felt was relief. Relief and joy. Within a few minutes an ambulance had arrived. The Paramedics were there. Rosie's foot was re-examined and just to be on the safe side she and her dad were taken to the nearest hospital.

'Just as a precaution' the ambulance crew said. 'If a child has been lost this is standard procedure.' So, like it or not Rosie had to go!

Rosie

Rosie was exhausted and for most of the journey to the hospital, she slept. The relieved searchers had all gone home with the exception of Mr Harries and Charlie.

They would have left too but Rosie's dad had asked if Bob and Charlie, for everyone was on first names by now, could stay at his house until he got back. 'I'm hoping we won't be too long and then I'll run you and Charlie back to the Jenkins' to collect your car.'

At Rosie's, Charlie had been made a fuss of, towelled dry, and given a few biscuits he lay there thinking. Processing humans call it!
Rosie's father had phoned from the hospital to pass on the news that she was fine. Rosie's mum relayed the message to Bob Harries who was waiting at the house a hot cup of tea in his hand.

At A & E it was a fairly quiet night for once and Rosie was next to be seen. So, it was not too long before she was checked out and told it was fine for her to go home.

Once there, hugged and kissed almost to death by her mum, as Rosie said later, she was bathed, dressed in clean warm pyjamas and dressing gown and given a cup of hot chocolate and food. Her mum and dad asked her why she had run away.

'Never ever do that again. Promise. Your dad and I were worried sick' said her mum.
'I'm sorry' said Rosie shaking her head. 'but I had to see Charlie one last time to let him know how much I loved him. I had to do it.'
Her father was silent.
As for Charlie, he was feeling very proud – he had found Rosie - ok with a little help but he was the one who had saved the day. His nose had stopped twitching and he felt his little heart fill with joy.

'This is what I was born to do' he thought.
This was his job. He felt a deep sense of contentment.

Partings

Rosie's dad looked at Mr Harries. 'Bob, I hadn't realised just how much Rosie loved Charlie. I know you have bought him but would you change your mind and let me buy him from you?'

Bob Harries was quiet as Rosie and her dad looked at him. Then he said quietly 'Charlie is incredible. He has all the makings of a wonderful search and rescue dog even though he has never had any training. Think how much good he could do to help find people if he were properly trained.'

'What do you think Rosie? It's up to you?'
Rosie was quiet as she looked first at
Charlie who was sitting there, He was panting slightly, his tongue hanging out and what she thought was a smile on his face. She then looked at Mr Harries. 'I want what's best for Charlie' she said with tears in her eyes. 'I'd like to think he was saving others just as he saved me'. Everyone was silent. Her mother sniffed.

Tears were in her eyes as she kissed and hugged her daughter.

Bob Harries looked at Rosie, then he said 'just between us - if it turns out Charlie isn't suitable for search and rescue work, I'll let you know. How does that sound?' He then looked at Rosie's parents before continuing to speak. 'I know how fond of Charlie you are Rosie and if your mum and dad agree how would you all like to come and see Charlie occasionally, and myself and the search and rescue team? That way you can keep in touch with what Charlie is doing. What do you think?'

Rosie's face lit up as she turned to her parents who nodded. 'Yes please' she said.

Charlie's New Life

By now it was getting late. Bob Harries finished his tea, and said that it was time he and Charlie were going.

He explained it was a long journey home and he couldn't feed Charlie before they got there. He didn't want him perhaps being sick in the car along the narrow, twisty Welsh roads especially in the dark. He picked up his backpack and slipped on Charlie's lead.

Rosie's mum looked at her husband then said 'Bob, we'd love it if you would have a meal with us and stay the night. That way you can feed Charlie and both of you can relax, have a good night's sleep and set off in the morning. We'll run you over to the Jenkins to pick up your car first thing'. Mr Harries gratefully accepted. It would also, he thought, give Rosie and Charlie a little more time together before they said goodbye. He knew Rosie's decision had been a hard one to make and hoped that his idea of the family visiting the Centre occasionally would lessen the blow of Charlie going.

So later that evening, Charlie lay down on the carpet in the lounge with Rosie beside him. He sighed. What a day it had been. He was tired but so very happy, He knew he had done well and his little nose twitched as he drifted off to sleep.

A new home. New beginnings. What more could he ask for?

About the Author

Stefanja, who writes as Steffi Gardner, is a native of Pembrokeshire. She lived and worded in the Midlands before returning to Pembrokeshire 17 years ago.

Apart from a wealth of short stories she has written various articles about animals and their emotions. She is a registered Bach Flower Practitioner, for both people and animals, and this is her first children's book.

Dogs have been an essential part of Steffi's life for as long as she can remember; her first being a Miniature Schnauzer called Sophie. Since then there have been other Minis, a Giant Schnauzer, Maisie, and a Golden

Retriever called Tally.

In October 2019 there was an unexpected addition to the family, a 7year old ex puppy farm dog named Harry. Read how Tally in FOR LOVE OF HARRY helped the extremely traumatised Harry start to live a new life.